Lila Grey, Let Go of the Day

*For Mom, for giving me the idea
and encouragement to write this book
and for my own L.G.,
you will always be my best gift.*

Written by Autumn Radle

Illustrated by Marrieta Gal

Painted Cave
Publishing

"Tell us one more story, please, Mama?
Falcon and I aren't sleepy yet.
Bedtime came too soon."

"All right my love,
just one more."

"This is *your* story, Lila Grey.
A tale of marvelous adventure,
as we travel through your busy day."

"You begin your day as a builder of cities,
a creator of plazas and parks:
a designer of dreams.

You are an **ARCHITECT**.

Blocks and boards of
thick or thin, tall or small,
you find value
and strength in all."

"Stack, steady, and slide.
Sometimes walls tumble
and plans fail,
but you keep going,
keep trying,
knowing success
is but one part
of your journey."

"Itching for freedom
and fresh air,
you dash outside.
You slosh across a creek,
leaping between the mossy
logs and lush ferns
you find there.

You are
an **EXPLORER.**
Dazzled by majestic
birch and maple,
you slow down
and listen to
nature's music."

"A visitor in this forest, you take time and appreciate the beauty all around. And you are careful not to disturb all of those you found: smooth green snake, red fox, and white-tailed deer.

Each plays a starring role in their own life's adventure, just like you.

Through days and nights, through sounds and sights, through discoveries, big and small; our stories intertwine us all."

Sprinting home,
you hold tight to
the images
of your day
now drawn in
your memory.

Pulling your easel
onto the porch,
you are eager to
capture the wonder
of the
sun-flecked woods.

Sketching,
painting,
creating,
you are
an **ARTIST**.

You are bold and expressive, transforming an empty canvas into a bright, magical landscape: sparkling emerald, shimmering violet, and bursts of lady slipper pink.

In these splashes of color, you are inspired.

Until . . . a hungry dragon awakes, growling in your empty belly, sending you skipping inside the garden gate to harvest the day's bounty.

You are a **FARMER**, plucking snap peas, twisting banana peppers off their prickly stems, pulling up rainbow carrots, and gently tugging cherry tomatoes from their spindly vines.

You gather them in the basket of your shirt, grateful because vegetables grown at home always taste better.

Bustling into the kitchen, you are a **CHEF** today.

Stepping onto your stool to reach the counter, you spy Daddy smiling in the doorway.

He is happy to be your assistant.

You line up the garden's gifts,
and then, step-by-step:
wash, chop, mix, and fold.

With Daddy's help,
you prepare *Lila Grey's
Vibrant Veggie Wraps,*
a fresh and crunchy
feast to share.

Trading in your chef's hat for western wear,
you gallop across the meadow.
A wrangler, brave and strong.
You are a **COWGIRL**.

Singing into the wind,
you hear the echoes of children from long ago
celebrating the joy of outdoor play.

With no screens, cords or batteries,
you heed the lessons of solitude,
how to be *alone*, but not *lonely*.

The horizon before you, cantering
to the melodies of goldfinches
and scarlet tanagers,
hints of honeysuckle
and lilac follow you home.

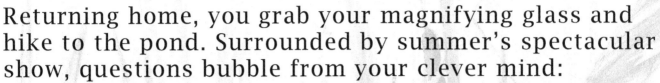

Returning home, you grab your magnifying glass and hike to the pond. Surrounded by summer's spectacular show, questions bubble from your clever mind:

Do butterflies have noses?
  No, but they can 'smell' with their feet.

Do frogs drink water?
  No, they absorb water through their skin.

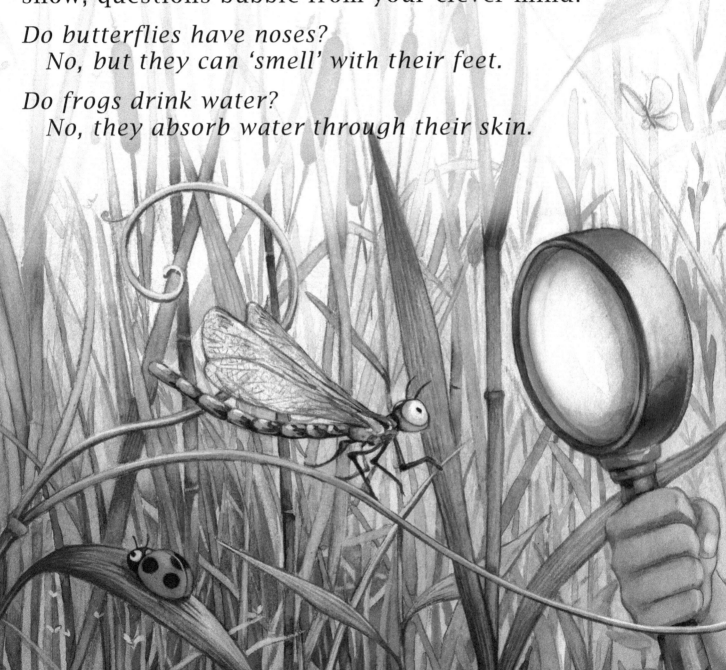

You are a **SCIENTIST**, searching for answers, untangling mysteries, and testing ideas. Your eyes twinkle with excitement, welcoming the challenges and discoveries ahead.

Looking up from the cattails and water lilies,
you see your neighbor, Luca.
With his head on his knees and tears on his cheeks,
you worry his hurt is too difficult to mend, but you
are determined to try.

You wrap your arm around his shoulder, and you wait. You listen. With kindness and patience, you are a **FRIEND**, helping him stand tall and believe in himself again.

You show that a tender heart is not weak, because your empathy is powerful.

Hearing my call to dinner, you invite Luca to join us,
certain that tamale night would cheer him.
Reunited around the sturdy oak table,
we share the stories of our day.

You are part of a **FAMILY**, built on a foundation of trust and forgiveness. Together we create a home: a place to laugh, to talk, to solve problems, to reflect, and be thankful.

Wishing Luca good night, you take the helm with the setting sun. Courageous and honest, you are a **CAPTAIN**, a leader of the evening voyage.

Inventing new quests among the bubbles, you search for mythical sea creatures and protect enchanted treasures from greedy pirates' hands.

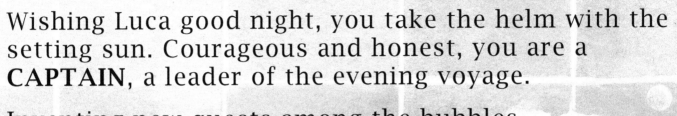

You spin these masquerades from glittering fantasy
until it is time to drop anchor and embrace
the warmth of a fluffy towel as you begin
to drift towards slumber.

And now my love, my Lila Grey,
it's time to let go of the day,
to tuck away these memories,
hold dear these triumphs,
and make room for what
tomorrow will bring.

Close your eyes and imagine
all you will do, and all
you will see. On your next
great adventure, what
will you be?

An astronaut?
A musician?
An engineer?

Whoever you will be, and whatever you will do,
keep discovering. Find the joy, be your own hero,
and make yourself proud.

You are a **GIFT**.

About the Author

AUTUMN RADLE grew up in the wilds of Upstate New York where she spent her free time exploring the forest and creek behind her house and reading as many books as she could carry home from the library.

After winning the classic children's picture book, Shel Silverstein's *The Giving Tree,* in Mrs. Rajczkewski's third grade poetry contest, Autumn's dream of becoming a writer began to take shape.

Practicality won out for a while, however, and Autumn dedicated the first half of her professional life to urban planning and sustainability, helping communities protect and enjoy nature while promoting environmental conservation.

Finally, ready to pursue her childhood dream, *Lila Grey, Let Go of the Day*, is Autumn's first picture book and was inspired by her own daughter's struggles to settle down to sleep after a busy day.

When she's not writing about Lila Grey's next adventure, you can find Autumn hiking in the mountains or enjoying time with her husband, daughter, two Great Pyrenees rescue dogs, and a rather persnickety cat.

CPSIA information can be obtained
at www.ICGtesting.com
Printed in the USA
LVHW071020180121
676463LV00020B/292

10